SIAN BESSEY

KIDS ON A
MISSION

ESCAPE
FROM GERMANY

Published by Covenant Communications, Inc.
American Fork, Utah

Printed in Canada
First Printing: May 2004

12 11 10 09 08 07 06 05 04   10 9 8 7 6 5 4 3 2 1

ISBN 1-59156-436-0

SIAN BESSEY

KIDS ON A
MISSION

ESCAPE FROM GERMANY

A NOVEL BY

SIAN BESSEY

Covenant

Covenant Communications, Inc.

*To dedicated teachers
who devote their lives to instilling a love
of reading in their young students*

And to my very own Matthew

CHAPTER 1

"Not again!" Matt groaned.

He kicked a tuft of grass in frustration. Ever since his best friend, Jon Packer, moved away, Matt Williams had been playing soccer alone. He'd just aimed a perfect shot at the goal—right between the garage door and the drainpipe—but without a goalie, the ball had bounced hard and sailed right over his backyard wall.

Matt headed for the large ash tree at the corner of his yard. It was an easy tree to climb and the best way up and over the wall that separated his back-yard from the Missionary Training Center in Provo, Utah. He'd climbed it often to retrieve a ball, or a Frisbee, or a kite. He and Jon had sometimes climbed it just to sit and watch the missionaries. But Matt hadn't done that for a few weeks now. It wasn't as much fun without a buddy.

It took only a few minutes for Matt to reach the branch that hung over the wall. He scrambled into a sitting position and peered down through the leaves, hunting for the missing soccer ball.

He spotted it almost immediately. It was lying directly below him, beside the old wooden shed on the MTC grounds.

But the ball wasn't the only thing Matt noticed. Puzzled, he stared at the shed. A strange blue light was seeping out through the cracks around the wooden door. He'd looked down at the shed hundreds of times, but he'd never seen any kind of light on. He'd never even seen anyone enter or leave the shed before.

Matt tried scooting forward along the branch. Then he moved back again to lean against the tree trunk. It didn't matter what angle he tried; the strange blue light remained.

Several missionaries passed by, but not one seemed to notice anything unusual about the nearby shed. Matt began to wonder if he were imagining things.

The gently moving leaves above his head shaded Matt from the sun, and he didn't feel terribly hot. Was seeing blue light a sign of heatstroke? He felt his forehead. He didn't think he was ill. He tried squinting. Then he closed his eyes, counted to ten, and opened them up again. No matter what he did, the strange blue light still glowed eerily below him.

Matt sat quietly, watching the last of the missionaries enter a distant building. Then, unable to contain his curiosity any longer, he inched his way along the branch until he could touch the wall. With a quick glance to make sure that there was still no one in sight, Matt climbed onto the top of the wall and started crawling forward.

"Does Mom know you're up there?" a voice called from his backyard.

Matt froze, with one knee already off the wall, and slowly turned to see his older sister staring up at him from beside the ash tree.

"Emily!" he hissed. "Go away!"

"Not till you tell me what you're doing," Emily said, folding her arms across her chest.

"Nothing," Matt said. "I'm just getting my ball."

"Yeah, right! Since when has getting your ball meant creeping around like a spy?" she asked.

Matt groaned and rolled his eyes. He wondered if Emily had some kind of "little brother radar" hidden in her long brown hair. She always seemed to show up at the worst possible times, and he knew she wouldn't leave until she was convinced he had nothing to hide. He scanned the MTC grounds and the windows of his own home. Satisfied that no one else was watching, he turned back to Emily.

"Climb the tree," he called down in a loud whisper.

Emily looked puzzled, as though she couldn't quite believe that Matt was giving in so easily. Then she hurried over to the ash tree and began climbing.

"Okay," Matt said when Emily reached the branch across from the wall. "Now, look down at the shed . . . right there . . . and tell me what you see."

Emily was quiet for a few seconds. "There's a weird bluish light coming out from under the door," she finally said.

"Check again—one eye at a time."

"Maaatt!" Emily complained, but she put a hand over her right eye, looked at the shed, then repeated the process with her left eye. "I can still see it. With both eyes," she announced.

"All right!"

Emily had better eyesight than anyone Matt knew. He was sure it had something to do with the fact that her eyes were different colors. If you looked closely, you could tell that one of her eyes was blue and the other was

6

green. If Emily could see the light with both eyes, it had to be real.

"Where's it coming from?" Emily asked.

"That is exactly what I'm going to find out."

"But you can't go down there," Emily said. "It could be dangerous."

"Em, it's okay." Matt began crawling forward again. "I've got to go down to get my soccer ball anyway."

"Matt!" Emily cried. "Matt, get back here!"

Matt ignored her. Now that he knew he wasn't imagining the blue light, he was even more eager to find out what it was.

When he reached the place where the shed roof almost touched the wall, he crouched and jumped. His feet made a loud clatter as they hit the tiles. He kept his head low, waiting to see if anyone would come out of the shed. No one came. The only sound was the rustling of leaves behind him.

Matt turned around. The tree branch was swaying wildly. Emily had just leaped onto the wall and was crawling toward him.

"Wait, Matt," she called. "If you're really going to do something this crazy, someone needs to be there to make sure you don't kill yourself."

"Oh great, thanks a lot!" Matt said.

"I'm serious," Emily said.

"Yeah, well all the noise you're making is going to get me into more trouble than climbing down from this shed roof ever will."

Matt slithered down the roof and dropped off the edge. He landed on the ground with a thump and cautiously approached the door. This close to the shed, the light seemed more white than blue, but it was still streaming out around the doorway. He stood before the door and wiped his sweating palms on his dark green T-shirt.

A solid thud followed by a muffled cry made Matt jump. He swung around as Emily appeared at the corner of the shed.

"You didn't need to follow me," Matt said.

Emily didn't answer. She brushed the grass off her knees and looked over at the shed. "Have you tried the door yet?" she asked.

Matt stopped thinking about his pesky sister and turned to face the door again. "No, I was just about to," he said.

He moved over to the door and grasped the handle. He could sense Emily right behind him. Slowly, he turned the knob in his hand. It moved.

"I think it's unlocked," he whispered over his shoulder.

Carefully, Matt turned the doorknob farther and gently pushed the door—just a few inches. Then he stopped, took a deep breath, and pushed the door a little more. Silently, it swung wide open.

CHAPTER 2

To the children's astonishment, the shed was almost completely dark inside. It smelled musty, as though no one had used it for a long time. Away in the shadowy corners they could make out the shapes of shovels, rakes, and hoes. There were some sacks, wooden stakes, and gardening gloves stacked on shelves across from where they stood.

Lying on an old, wooden desk beside the shed wall was what looked like a long, thin piece of paper. It was glowing with the same bright light they'd seen from the ash tree.

"What is it?" Emily whispered.

"I don't know," Matt replied.

He stepped into the shed and moved closer. Emily followed him.

"Close the door," Matt said. "Just in case someone comes this way."

Emily turned and closed the door. Immediately the light from the paper on the desk filled the small shed.

"It looks like an envelope," Matt said, "and there's something written on the front."

Emily leaned forward for a closer look. "It says *Brother and Sister Williams*."

"That's us!" Matt gasped. "The envelope's for us."

"Yeah, right," Emily said. "It could be for anyone with the same last name—even Mom and Dad."

"No way! It has to be us, Em. Not one of the missionaries who passed the shed took a look at it. It was like they couldn't even see the light. But I saw it as soon as I climbed the tree. And so did you, didn't you?"

"Yeeesss," Emily said slowly.

"See, that proves it," Matt said.

"That doesn't prove anything," Emily began, but Matt was already reaching for the envelope.

He tore it open and pulled out a single sheet of paper. As he did so, two thin, black squares of plastic fell from the envelope and landed on the desk. Matt picked them up and turned them over in his hand.

"They're missionary name tags," Matt said. "Look."

Emily peered at the tags in Matt's hand. One said *Sister Williams*, and the other said *Brother Williams*.

Underneath the names were the words *The Church of Jesus Christ of Latter-day Saints.*

"What're they for?" Emily asked, picking up the one that said *Sister Williams.*

Matt just stared at the piece of paper in his other hand. "Cool!" he said, his eyes bright with excitement. "You're not going to believe this." He thrust the letter at Emily. "We've been called on a mission to Germany."

"Very funny!" Emily said.

She glanced at the paper in her hand. It was an official-looking letter addressed to Brother Matthew and Sister Emily Williams. After skimming through the beginning of the letter, she reached a part that said, *You have been called to serve in the West German Mission.*

Emily handed the letter back to Matt. "But Matt, this doesn't make any sense. I'm only eleven and you're nine. Kids don't go on missions."

"Well, they don't see weird blue lights coming out of old sheds either, and that happened." Matt looked back at the letter. It was signed, *Heber J. Grant.* Stunned, he read it again to be sure. Heber J. Grant. He was the prophet of the Church ages ago. He checked the top of the letter for a date. *August 27, 1939.*

"Em, did you see when this letter was written?" Matt's voice was not much more than a squeak.

"No," Emily said.

"August 27, 1939. And it's signed by President Heber J. Grant."

"What?" Emily snatched the letter back from Matt's hands.

Matt pointed to the prophet's signature at the bottom of the piece of paper.

"Isn't that cool?" he asked.

"Cool? Is that all you can say?"

"Okay then, it's awesome!" Matt said happily.

"But I don't get it? What does it mean?"

"Oh, come on, Em. Stop trying to figure everything out. We'll have plenty of time for that when we're home. Let's put these name tags on."

With a sigh, Emily put the letter down on the desk and glanced at the black name tag in her other hand. Matt was already pinning his onto his green T-shirt. She shrugged her shoulders. She knew Matt wouldn't stop pestering her until she had hers on too. Quickly, she attached it to her purple shirt.

Suddenly the bright light in the shed swirled around and around, and a low-pitched humming filled the small room. Then—just as suddenly—it stopped.

Emily looked over at Matt. "This is getting too weird. Let's go," she said.

Matt looked around the shed. Nothing seemed different, and yet . . .

"Okay," he said and walked over to the door. Carefully, he opened it a couple of inches and peeked outside.

A shrill whistle sounded. Smoke filled the air. People were everywhere—moving rapidly past the doorway and talking or shouting in another language.

Matt slammed the door shut and leaned against it. "Uh, how about we do that figuring out now, after all?"

"What's wrong?" Emily asked. "Is someone out there?"

"You . . . you could say that," Matt said.

"What do you mean? Either there is someone there or there isn't."

Matt moved away from the door. "You look."

Emily grasped the doorknob and carefully turned it. She opened the door a crack and put her eye to the opening. Then she closed it almost as fast as Matt had.

"Matt, what did you do?" she cried.

"Nothing!" Matt said. "All I did was open the door. You saw me."

"This is crazy," Emily said. "Those people out there . . . I think they're speaking German!"

Matt stared back at her, his face especially pale in the bluish light. "D'you think we've been sent on our mission?"

Emily took a deep breath. "Okay, this has to be a dream, and I'm going to wake up any minute."

Matt reached over and gave his sister's arm a good pinch.

"Ouch! What was that for?" Emily cried.

"Well," Matt said, "now you know you're not dreaming."

Emily looked over at the door with wide, frightened eyes. "Then what're we going to do?" she whispered.

"We could stay in here and hope no one finds us," Matt suggested.

"For the rest of our lives?" Emily said with panic in her voice.

"I don't think so. Mission calls don't last forever. Maybe there's something we need to do here, and once it's done, we'll go back home."

"How?" Emily asked.

Matt shrugged. "I don't know, exactly."

He picked up the envelope. It was still glowing, but far less brightly than earlier. "It has to have something to do with this." He looked over at his sister. "Maybe, once we're out there, we'll know what we need to do."

Emily watched Matt replace the envelope on the table.

"All right," she said, chewing her lower lip. She always bit her lip when she was nervous. "We'll try going out—but don't do anything stupid!"

"I won't, if you won't," Matt said, and before Emily could change her mind, he turned, opened the shed door, and stepped outside.

CHAPTER 3

Matt and Emily were immediately swallowed up by the crowd. They pushed their way back to the wall and huddled together, watching the people swirl around them. Men, women, and children moved back and forth in every direction—and they didn't look like the people at home. The women all wore dresses or skirts. Their hair was either long and loose or pulled up into a bun or ponytail, and almost all of them wore hats. The men were in hats too, and they wore button-down shirts with black, gray, or brown pants. There was not a single brightly colored T-shirt or pair of jeans to be seen.

Emily looked down at her own clothes and cringed. "We're not dressed like them," she whispered. "I'm the only girl not wearing a dress. They're going to think I'm a boy!"

Matt glanced over at Emily. Her brown hair was pulled back into a ponytail with a purple elastic—exactly the same color as her purple shirt.

"You'll be fine," he said. "Boys don't wear ponytails." He turned and focused on the scene before them. "I've never seen anything like this before. Where are we?"

Everyone looked worried. Even though Matt and Emily didn't know what was wrong, they could feel the tension. Some people walked by slowly. Some ran. Some were so tired and weak that they had to be helped by others to walk. People were calling out to family members or friends and yelling for direction or help. A few were crying.

"Matt, look at these people," Emily whispered. "They're all so sad. Something must really be wrong."

"But what?" Matt asked.

His eyes widened as two men approached wearing khaki brown uniforms and carrying heavy backpacks and large guns. Their heads were covered by hard helmets, shaped almost like upside down bowls. They walked right past Matt and Emily without even glancing their way. Matt and Emily watched them as the crowd parted to let the two men through.

"German soldiers," Matt said in a hushed tone. "I recognize their uniforms. They're just like the ones on my

Conquering Heroes computer game. World War II German infantry."

"What are they . . . ?" Emily began.

"D'you remember the date on the mission call?" Matt interrupted.

Emily thought for a moment. "1939. I think it was August 1939," she said.

"Yes. And World War II began in 1939," Matt said. "1939 to 1944. It lasted almost five years. We've arrived in Germany right at its beginning."

Emily knew Matt had a great memory for numbers—especially dates—but even so, she was amazed. "How do you know all that?" she asked, her eyes wide.

Matt shrugged. "*Conquering Heroes.* I've told you before that you could learn stuff playing that game."

Any response Emily could have made was drowned out by a piercing whistle. Both children clapped their hands over their ears. Puffs of smoke and hissing steam billowed upward. Emily and Matt stared through the narrow gap in the crowd created by the passing soldiers and saw what lay beyond. For the first time, the children realized that they were standing on a large platform. Just a few yards away, at the platform's edge, was a huge, black train.

The children's view of the train was quickly blocked by the mass of people all pressing forward, desperately trying to climb on board. Officials were pushing them away—there was no more room.

They watched as a family with two young children stepped off the train to make room for the soldiers. As soon as the soldiers were on board there was another long whistle followed by the screeching of metal and the shunting of pistons. The train was leaving, and within minutes the sound of the train was faint in the distance.

Some of the people who had tried so hard to reach the train moved back a little and sat down heavily on their trunks and packages. But none of the people actually left the station—only more arrived.

The children were bumped and jostled. One really bad shove sent Matt sideways. Emily reached out and grabbed his T-shirt.

"Stay close," she said. "We shouldn't get separated."

Matt nodded and stuck right behind his sister as she fought her way toward the station entrance, where the crowd was thinner. When she finally stopped, Emily leaned against the brick wall and turned to face Matt.

"What're we going to do?" she asked.

"I don't know." Matt glanced at the name tag on his sister's shirt. "What would missionaries do?"

"Teach people about the Church, read the scriptures . . ." Emily shrugged.

"How about praying?" Matt said.

"Yes!" Emily cried. "Why didn't we think of that before? Say a prayer, Matt."

Matt didn't take time to argue. He bowed his head, closed his eyes, and in a soft voice he prayed that Heavenly Father would watch over them. Then he asked for help in knowing what he and Emily should do to return home safely.

It was a short prayer, but they both said amen with more feeling than they ever had before.

Emily gave a big sigh. "Okay, now what?"

Matt looked around. A boy entered the station pushing a large wooden cart. The cart was loaded so high that the boy couldn't see where he was going. He had to keep stopping to check for obstacles.

Following close behind the cart was an old woman walking with a cane. She was wearing a blue suit and matching hat with a feather flopping across the brim. Even from where he stood, Matt could see the sparkle of her many rings and necklaces.

She called out to the boy and waved her cane to a spot not far from where Matt and Emily stood. The boy veered the cart in that direction. When he brought it to a stop, he started heaving the first big trunk off the cart.

The woman leaned on her cane and watched the boy stagger under the weight of the luggage. She was more concerned about damage to the trunks than how hard it was for the boy to lift each piece.

When the boy set the second trunk down with a bang, the woman shouted at him.

Matt couldn't watch anymore. "Let's go help that kid over there," he suggested.

"What if he doesn't want our help?" Emily asked, hanging back.

"Who wouldn't want help hauling huge boxes like that?"

"Well, the old lady might not like it. She doesn't look very friendly. And besides, we've got to figure out what we're doing here before we do anything else."

"We could've stayed in the shed and done that!" Matt said with disgust. "You can stand here and figure everything out if you want. I'm going to do something useful."

He walked over to the cart, and since Emily was more concerned over being separated than over what Matt was doing, she followed him.

The boy looked up as they approached. The old woman stepped closer.

"Hi!" Matt said. "Can I help you?"

The boy looked at Matt in confusion.

"He's German, Matt," Emily whispered. "He probably can't understand you."

Matt paused. He signaled with his hands—first at the luggage, then at the floor. "Help you," he said, pointing to himself and then to the boy.

"Help?" the boy repeated, his face breaking into a smile. "Yes . . . thank you."

Matt grinned at Emily. "Told ya!"

He moved forward, but Emily grabbed his arm and pulled him back.

"Matt," she said, "you just spoke in German! That boy understood you, and what's even crazier—so did I!"

Matt stared at Emily. "You just spoke in German too!"

Emily clapped her hand to her mouth, and Matt laughed at the look on her face. Then he turned and picked up one end of the next trunk on the cart.

Immediately, the elderly woman started shouting and waving her cane. The boys put down the trunk, and Emily poked Matt in the ribs.

"See, I was right too," she said.

The German boy turned and spoke to the woman. He managed to persuade her that Matt and Emily weren't trying to steal anything, and she finally calmed down. But she inched closer to her luggage and watched the children like a hawk.

When at last the final piece of luggage was unloaded, the boy approached the woman.

She dug a couple of coins out of her purse and gave them to him. The boy then returned to Matt and Emily and offered one of the coins to them.

"No," Matt said, shaking his head. "No, you keep it." He noticed that patches had been sewn onto the knees of the boy's gray pants, and the buttons on his shirt didn't match. Matt guessed he needed the money.

"Thank you," the boy said. Then he pocketed the coins, lifted the handles of his wooden cart, and with a brief smile, disappeared into the crowd.

Matt didn't have time to think about the boy for long. Emily was tugging on his sleeve.

"Listen," she said. "Do you hear that?"

Matt pulled a face. "Em, I can hardly hear you, there's so much noise here."

"No," Emily said more urgently. "Try, Matt. Listen hard."

Matt turned his head and focused on the sounds around him. At first all he could hear was the babble of voices. But then, floating above the confusion of noise, he heard a clear whistle. Not the strident whistle of a train, but the soft, sweet whistle of music. Matt strained to hear the notes.

"'Do What Is Right,'" Matt breathed. "Someone's whistling 'Do What Is Right.'"

Emily nodded, excitement shining in her eyes. "Maybe there are other missionaries here," she said.

Matt grabbed her arm. "Come on. Let's try to find the person who's whistling."

CHAPTER 4

It ended up being easier to find the source of the whistling than Matt and Emily had imagined. The children wove through the crowd, trying to follow the general direction of the distant notes.

All at once, they saw him—a tall man in a dark suit and hat. He was standing on top of a large crate, high above the heads of the people nearby. He puckered up his lips and whistled "Do What Is Right" again. Then he anxiously scanned the crowd, as though he were looking for someone.

Within minutes, Matt and Emily had reached the crate. At the same time, two other men arrived. One was short, had black curly hair, and was dressed in a dark suit and hat too. The other one wore a brown jacket and pants. His hair was reddish brown, and he had a long, red mustache that curled upward at the corners of his mouth. He was carrying a bulging backpack.

The man in the dark suit called up to the tall man who was whistling. "Elder Blanchard! Elder Blanchard!"

Elder Blanchard, the tall man on the crate, looked down and smiled widely. He jumped off the crate and put his arms around the two men.

"Elder Wyatt! President Bohman! Boy, am I glad to see you!"

Matt waited until the tall man stepped back, then he reached out and touched his arm. "Excuse me," he said. "Are you missionaries for The Church of Jesus Christ of Latter-day Saints?"

The man looked at Matt with surprise. "Yes, we are. Well, Elder Wyatt and I are. President Bohman is the district president for the Church in this area." He paused then asked, "Who are you?"

Matt stuck out his hand. "I'm Matt Williams, and this is my sister, Emily." He took a deep breath, then continued on. "I know this sounds nuts, but we just received a mission call to Germany. We're not sure how we got here or what we need to do. Maybe you're supposed to help us . . . or we're supposed to help you . . . or something?"

"What Matt's trying to say," Emily interrupted, "is that we just arrived from the future. We went into a shed at the MTC, opened a glowing envelope, put on missionary tags, and walked out here."

The three men stared at the children.

"Oh, that was really good," Matt muttered.

"I was just trying to help them understand," Emily whispered back.

Matt rolled his eyes. "Em, we don't even understand—and we lived through it!"

Elder Wyatt cleared his throat. "You're . . . um . . . you're a bit young to be missionaries, aren't you?"

"That's what I thought too," Emily said quickly.

Elder Blanchard put his hand on Matt's shoulder. "All right, Brother Williams, why don't you and your sister come and sit on this crate and explain yourselves—from the beginning—no matter how crazy it seems."

Matt and Emily settled onto the crate.

"From the beginning?" Matt asked.

"From the beginning," Elder Blanchard repeated.

"Well, it all started when my soccer ball flew over the wall . . ." Matt told them the whole story, and by the time he finished, the men were looking even more stunned than when he'd begun.

Emily looked anxiously from one to the other. "Do you . . . do you believe us?"

"Er . . . I'm trying," Elder Wyatt said, looking over at Elder Blanchard with his eyebrows raised.

Elder Blanchard leaned forward. He had an excited sparkle in his eyes. "So, you're telling me that in the future, there's some sort of training place for missionaries?"

"Yeah," Matt said. "It's huge. Missionaries come from all over the world. They learn new languages and the missionary discussions before they go into the mission field."

"That's so fantastic! I was in Germany for months before I could understand a conversation between two people. But with a head start like that . . . wow!" Elder Blanchard shook his head in amazement. "But tell me one thing. Why is it called the *Empty Sea*?"

Matt and Emily looked at him blankly.

Then, all at once, Matt understood. "Oh, you mean the *M-T-C*." He said each letter clearly. "That stands for *Missionary Training Center*."

Elder Blanchard looked sheepish. "That makes more sense."

"So . . . so you do believe us?" Emily asked again.

Elder Blanchard sighed. "It's the most ridiculous story I've ever heard." As Matt's and Emily's shoulders sagged, he gave a small smile. "But it does explain your strange clothes and the fact that you speak German with an American accent."

"Then you'll help us?" Emily asked.

Elder Blanchard raised his hands. "I don't know what I can do. I'm here to help get missionaries out of Germany, but I have no idea how you are to leave—or where you're to go."

"Tell us again. What was the last thing you did before you found yourselves here?" Elder Wyatt asked.

The children thought for a moment.

"We put on our missionary name tags," Emily said.

"Perhaps you'll go back when you take them off again," Elder Wyatt suggested.

Matt and Emily looked at each other.

"Let's try it," Emily said.

Carefully, they both unpinned their black tags. Nothing happened. They held the tags in their hands and looked back at Elder Wyatt.

"We're still here," Matt announced.

The children pinned their name tags back onto their shirts.

"I wonder," said President Bohman thoughtfully. "I wonder if taking off your tags is the answer, but only when the time is right. Perhaps whatever brought you here can only send you back when you've fulfilled your mission."

"Hey, I bet that's it," Elder Wyatt agreed.

"But how are we going to do that?" Emily asked. "Elder Blanchard said he's here to help all the missionaries leave Germany. We just arrived."

"Yeah. Why are the missionaries leaving, anyway?" Matt asked.

Elder Blanchard looked sad. "You've arrived in Germany at a very bad time, Brother Williams. For months there have been rumors that the man who leads this country, Adolf Hitler, is planning to invade neighboring countries. Hitler wants more power and more land. He has built a strong army, and we believe he is now ready to use it. Germany is preparing for war."

"That's why everyone here looks so scared and everything feels so . . . well . . . so bad," Matt said, not sure how to put his feelings into words.

Elder Blanchard pointed to the crowded railway platform. "All the people you see here want to leave. Many are trying to return to their families in other parts of the country. Others, especially our Jewish brothers and sisters, may be killed if they are unable to get away now.

"Some men, like President Bohman here, are being forced to leave their homes to join the military. And we American missionaries have just received a message from the prophet to be out of Germany within three days."

"But where are the missionaries to go?" Emily asked.

Elder Blanchard looked concerned. "There has been talk of war in Germany for a long time. Our mission president told us that if we ever had to evacuate the country, we should all travel as fast as possible to Holland and gather there.

"But now we have a big problem. The mission president has just learned that the guards at the border between Germany and Holland are not allowing anyone through. Our missionaries will be stranded. To make things worse, the telephone lines are down, and we have no way of knowing exactly where the missionaries are. But we must find them. Only a ticket to England or Denmark can get them out of Germany now."

Elder Blanchard patted his suit coat pocket. "I've been given the tickets and money they need. The mission president has asked me to find our missing missionaries."

"But how?" Matt asked. "They could be anywhere."

"Anywhere," Elder Blanchard agreed solemnly. "Anywhere between here and the border. I know there's no way I can do it alone. But with the Lord's help—"

"And ours," Matt interrupted. "Maybe that's why we're here. We can help you find the other missionaries."

Everyone stared at Matt—especially Emily.

"I mean it," he said when no one spoke. "We have to be here for a reason.

And you've already admitted that you need help."

"But, Matt," Emily said, "what can we do?"

"I think it's time we found out," Elder Blanchard said quietly. "Let's pray together."

Elder Blanchard offered a simple prayer, expressing love and faith and asking for strength and guidance. When the prayer was over, Matt and Emily felt a calming peace.

"So what do we do next?" Emily asked Elder Blanchard.

"Well, I think I'll have to take the next train—wherever it's headed. I'll get off at other stations and try whistling again."

"It worked for us," Elder Wyatt said.

"And us too," Matt said.

Elder Blanchard smiled. "Well, perhaps it'll work again."

"You'll be lucky to get on a train," President Bohman pointed out. "They're not running on schedule anymore, and they're all full."

"I know," Elder Blanchard said, "but the prophet said that all the missionaries are to leave Germany, so I'm sure the Lord will provide a way for me to find them."

President Bohman nodded. "You will find them. But before you leave here, we must be sure that all missionaries in this city are found."

Elder Blanchard turned to Elder Wyatt. "Where's your companion?"

"I don't know where Elder Harris is," said Elder Wyatt. "We had to separate when we left our apartment.

"I took all the branch records to President Bohman. He was leaving for the station, so we walked here together. But Elder Harris went to help Elder and Sister Olsen. We were supposed to meet here, but I haven't seen them yet."

Elder Blanchard put his hand into his pocket and pulled out a slip of paper, which he handed to Elder Wyatt.

"Here's your ticket, Elder Wyatt," he said. "I'm going to stay here on this crate, and I'll keep whistling 'Do What Is Right' until the train arrives. You and President Bohman split up and whistle the same tune down each end of the station. If Elder Harris and the Olsens are here, surely one of us will find them, and I can give tickets to them before it's too late."

"What about us?" Matt asked.

Before Elder Blanchard could reply, they heard someone shout.

The missionaries turned to see a boy with a baggage cart standing just a few feet away.

Matt and Emily recognized him immediately. It was the same boy they'd helped earlier.

"Hey!" he shouted. "Are you looking for the other missionaries?"

"Yes," Elder Blanchard said. "Do you know where they are?"

The boy nodded excitedly. "I will show you. I know the house."

Elder Blanchard stepped closer to the boy and spoke to him.

Matt and Emily watched as the boy nodded his understanding and glanced over at them a few times.

Finally, Elder Blanchard turned to Matt and Emily.

"This is Otto," he said. "He knows Elder and Sister Olsen, and he can take you to the house where they are staying.

"Would you go with him? See if you can find them and Elder Harris—

and bring them back here as fast as you can."

Emily looked at Matt nervously, but when he said, "We'll go," she nodded.

Elder Blanchard dug deep into his pocket and took out three coins. He handed them to Matt. "Take these," he said. "In case of an emergency. If you're not able to find the missionaries within two hours, come back here."

Emily glanced at her watch. It was nine thirty. "We'll be back by eleven thirty," she said.

"Eleven thirty," Matt repeated.

Emily knew he was filing the deadline away in that special place in his brain reserved for memorized numbers.

Elder Blanchard shook Matt's hand then Emily's. "Follow the promptings of the Spirit," he said. "It's our only hope."

"We'll be back soon," Matt called. Then he and Emily ran to catch up with Otto, who was already pushing his cart through the crowd toward the station entrance.

CHAPTER 5

Walking out of the railway station was like walking into another world. Gone were the crowds, the shouting, and the pushing. Instead, Matt and Emily followed Otto onto a quiet street lined with tall, old stone buildings. The roads were empty. Not a single car was in sight. The few people they passed were hurrying toward the station.

Otto turned once and beckoned. "Come," he called.

Matt and Emily quickened their pace until they were walking alongside him.

Otto led them down a narrow street that meandered through rows and rows of old houses and offices. Red flags with crooked black crosses in the center hung from the buildings. The sun shone down brightly, and a solitary bird sang from one of the large, shady trees that they passed.

It should have felt like a beautiful summer morning at home.

But it didn't.

There was a feeling in the air, something that Matt and Emily couldn't really understand, something that was not right.

"Where is everyone?" Emily asked.

Otto shrugged. "Some are gone already. The men go to fight. The women, the children, the old men—they stay in their houses or they go for food."

"But there aren't any cars," Matt said.

"The soldiers have all the fuel," Otto said. "If people still have cars now, they cannot drive them. There is no gasoline."

Matt and Emily looked at each other. They were each thinking of the two shiny cars that sat in their garage at home. They'd never had to worry about not having enough gas. They'd never even thought about it.

"Come," Otto said again. "We are close."

He ran across the street, pushing the baggage cart as he went. Matt and Emily followed as Otto led them to a gray stone house squeezed in between other gray stone houses. A few dusty pink flowers bloomed in window boxes on either side of the dark brown door. Otto glanced up and down the street, then turned and knocked.

The three children waited. At first there was no sign of anyone, then the lace curtain in a window above their heads twitched. Otto saw it and knocked on the door again. Footsteps sounded, drawing nearer. Matt and Emily watched nervously as the door slowly opened. A dark-haired, dark-eyed woman peered out at them.

The door was open little more than a crack when she began to speak. Even though Matt and Emily couldn't hear what she was saying, they could tell that she was afraid and did not want them there. Otto stepped forward and began talking in a soft, urgent tone. Finally she shook her head and looked at Matt and Emily.

"The Americans are not here," she said. "Go. Go now. Do not come back." Then she closed the door firmly in their faces.

"We must go," Otto said, and he began pushing his cart away from the house as quickly as he could. Matt and Emily had to run to keep up with him.

"Otto," Emily said, a little out of breath. "What's wrong? What happened at the house?"

"Shhh," Otto said. "First we must go."

Otto didn't speak again until they turned onto another road, one that opened into a row of small shops. Finally, they were among other people again. But the people weren't wandering in and out of the stores, chatting with their neighbors. They were quietly standing in three long lines.

"What are these people waiting for?" Emily asked.

"For food," Otto said. "Bread . . . potatoes . . . fish. There may not be enough today. But they wait and they hope."

Emily noticed that there were only women, children, and old men in line.

"We must join the line," Otto said.

Matt glanced at his watch. "We don't have time to wait for food. We have to meet Elder Blanchard at the railway station, and we still haven't found the other missionaries."

"First we will stand with these people," Otto insisted, and without waiting to hear more protests, he took his place in the nearest line.

When Matt and Emily reluctantly moved up beside him, Otto spoke again.

"Stay here," he whispered. "I will hide the cart." And suddenly he was gone.

Emily looked at Matt with panic in her eyes. "Where did he go?" she said.

Matt leaned forward, searching for any sign of Otto. "I don't know. But I sure hope he comes back."

Matt had barely said the words when Otto appeared beside them.

"Boy, are we glad to see you!" Matt said.

Otto grinned, then with a quick glance back in the direction they had come, he was suddenly serious.

"I took the cart to a friend's house. Three children with a cart are too easy to find." He pointed to the other children in the line where they now stood. "Three children with many other children are not so easy."

"What do you mean?" Emily asked.

"The Gestapo are watching the missionaries' house," Otto said. "Now they will watch us."

"What are the Gestapo?" Matt asked.

"The Gestapo are the secret police. They work for Germany's leader, Adolph Hitler. They are suspicious of anyone who does not do things the way Hitler wants. The Gestapo watch the missionaries because the missionaries do not follow Hitler. Then they watch anyone who is a friend to the missionaries."

"Is that why the lady at the house was so scared and wouldn't let us in?" Emily asked.

Otto nodded. "She knows the Gestapo watch her and her house because the Olsens were staying there. She is afraid for what they might do."

"Well, what could they do?" Matt asked. "She hasn't done anything wrong."

Otto shrugged. "The Gestapo have great power, and they are very cruel. They do not need a reason to destroy a person's life. They take pleasure in it."

A shiver ran down Emily's spine. She looked over her shoulder, back down the street they'd walked through just minutes ago. It still seemed empty.

"You think they're watching us now?" she asked.

"I think they followed us," Otto said. "But I do not know if they still watch."

"We've got to find the missionaries and go back to the station," Matt said, trying not to sound frightened.

"Yes, but they are no longer at the home," Otto said. "I do not know where they are."

Emily and Matt looked at each other. "I think we need to pray again," Emily said.

"Here?" asked Otto with surprise.

"Here," said Matt firmly.

Matt and Emily bowed their heads and quietly prayed for help in finding the missionaries and getting back to the railway station safely.

When they raised their heads, Otto was watching them. "You truly believe God will help you?" he asked.

"Yes," Emily said. "He will help us. We're doing His work."

Otto looked down and kicked a small rock. "I do not know if I believe in God."

He looked so sad that Matt reached out and touched his arm. "It's okay, Otto," Matt said. "Even if you're not sure how you feel about Him right now, Heavenly Father still loves you. He loves everyone."

Otto looked at the hungry people standing in the line with them and shook his head. "The Olsens visited my home often. They taught us about your church. When they spoke about a God who loves us, it felt good. But now, when I see what is happening to our friends and neighbors, it is very hard to believe."

"Everyone has times when they feel sad or scared or mad. And this," Emily said, pointing to the lines of people, "is a very bad time. But when you believe in God, even though the bad things don't disappear right away, some of the pain inside does."

Otto sighed. "Perhaps," he said. "Perhaps I will try harder to believe."

He looked up and gave Matt and Emily a small smile, then his attention was drawn to a gray-haired man who was limping out of the shop with one small loaf of bread in his hand. Otto's smile grew bigger.

"Maybe now I really do believe," he said. "Come! Quick! That man is Elder Olsen."

CHAPTER 6

The three children ran across the road and caught up with Elder Olsen as he reached the corner.

"Elder Olsen!" Otto called.

The gray-haired man stopped and turned to meet them.

"Otto!" he said, greeting the boy with a firm handshake.

Then Matt stepped up. "Elder Olsen," he said, "I'm Matt Williams, and this is my sister, Emily. Elder Blanchard sent us. He's waiting at the railway station with tickets for you and Sister Olsen and Elder Harris."

Matt looked down at his watch. "We need to meet him back at the station as soon as we can."

Elder Olsen's eyes shone. "Brother Williams," he said, shaking Matt's hand. "You're an answer to prayer—but we must hurry."

Elder Olsen's limp hardly slowed him down at all. The children followed him past two buildings then down a small, dark alley. Little sunlight filtered in between the tall roofs, and the air felt cold and damp. A couple of cats were hiding in the shadows. Emily jumped when one of the cats brushed against her legs.

Elder Olsen finally stopped beside a green wooden door. He knocked softly. Matt and Emily noticed Otto glancing up and down the alley while they waited. They found themselves watching nervously too.

After what seemed like a very long time, they heard a bolt being pulled back, and slowly the door opened. A young man with sandy blond hair and thick-rimmed glasses looked out at them. When he saw Elder Olsen, he opened the door wide. As soon as they'd all entered, the young man closed the door and pushed the lock back into place.

Three large trunks were lying on the floor just inside the door. Elder Olsen stepped around them. The children sat down, one on each trunk, grateful to rest for a few minutes.

"Glad you're back safely, Elder Olsen," the young man said. "Who are these young people?"

"Elder Harris, let me introduce my old friend Otto," said Elder Olsen, "and Brother and Sister Williams, who are here with a message from Elder Blanchard."

"Elder Blanchard is waiting for you at the railway station with tickets to help you out of the country," Matt explained.

"But he told us to be back by eleven thirty, so we don't have much time," Emily added.

"We must hurry then," Elder Olsen said. "Elder Harris, how is Sister Schmidt?"

"She's resting. Sister Olsen is with her," Elder Harris said. His glasses had slipped down his nose, and he pushed them back in place.

"I'll go and talk to them," Elder Olsen said, and with the small loaf of bread still in his hands, he headed up the stairs.

Elder Harris turned to the children. "We were on our way to the railway station when the Olsens received a message from Sister Schmidt. She has been very ill and needed a priesthood blessing. We came as quickly as we could. Elder Olsen and I gave her a blessing, but when Sister Olsen found out that there was no food in the house, she sent Elder Olsen to find some. She is very worried about leaving Sister Schmidt here alone—even though she knows that we must leave while we still can."

Otto looked thoughtful. "When my mother was not able to leave her bed, Sister Olsen cared for her and Elder Olsen brought us food. Perhaps now we can repay their kindness."

"What d'you mean?" Matt asked.

Otto didn't answer. He scrambled over the trunk and pushed back the bolt on the front door.

"Are you going back out there on your own?" Emily asked.

Otto smiled. "It is much harder for the Gestapo to find one boy alone than three children together—especially one boy who knows the streets better than they do. You will see. I shall return very soon."

Then, before anyone could say anything more, he slipped through the door and was gone.

"I wonder what that was all about," Elder Harris said, looking as puzzled as Matt and Emily felt.

"I don't know," Matt said. "But I hope he's okay out there."

Elder Harris moved over to the door and slid the bolt back into place.

"Otto told us about the Gestapo," Emily explained. "He said they were watching the Olsens' house and may have followed us too."

Elder Harris frowned. "They've been watching us for weeks now. Some missionaries have been taken in for questioning or have had their papers taken."

"What kind of papers?" Matt asked.

"Passports, visas—the papers that allowed us into Germany. They even take Church paperwork sometimes— just to check it out. They look for any excuse to have us arrested," Elder Harris replied.

Matt gave his watch another look, then quickly raised his eyes to Elder Harris's face at the sound of firm, heavy footsteps halting on the other side of the door. Elder Harris heard it too. He put his finger to his lips and dug his other hand into his pocket. Pulling out a small set of keys, he moved over to the trunks.

"Quick!" he whispered. "Get inside and don't make a sound." He unlocked the nearest trunk and pulled open the lid.

Without a word, Emily and Matt stepped into the dark wooden trunk.

Emily could see fear in Matt's eyes, and she knew that it showed in her face too. She reached over and squeezed his hand just before Elder Harris lowered the lid.

The trunk was already half full of clothes and books. The children curled up as tightly as they could, and Elder Harris was almost able to close the lid.

"Not a sound!" he warned softly through the tiny crack. "No matter what happens, don't make a sound."

A huge bang shook the door. Something hard—a stick, a shoe, or perhaps a gun—was being pounded against it.

"Open up!" yelled a voice from the other side. "Gestapo! Open up!"

"Pray for us!" Elder Harris whispered, then he rose to his feet, and the children heard him walking across the tiled floor to the door.

They listened to the bolt being scraped back, then the door slammed open against the wall as the Gestapo officer pushed it out of his way.

"Your name?" the officer demanded, stepping into the house.

"Samuel Harris," came the reply.

"What are you doing here?" the officer asked.

"I'm a missionary for The Church of Jesus Christ of Latter-day Saints," Elder Harris said. "I'm here to minister to a member of our congregation."

"American!" The officer spat the words. "Give me your papers."

Matt and Emily strained to hear as the officer rustled through Elder Harris's papers. Very little fresh air was getting into the trunk. It was getting hotter and hotter, but neither of them dared to move or even to take a deep breath. Sweat ran down Matt's forehead. He let it drip into his eye without even raising a hand to brush it away. He just kept his eyes closed, praying with all his might that the Gestapo officer would not think to check the trunks and that he would leave before he and Emily suffocated inside.

"You are planning to leave?" The officer was talking again. "This is a lot of luggage for one missionary."

"The trunks are not all mine," Elder Harris said. "Other missionaries are already at the railway station. They are waiting for me and for the trunks."

Emily's racing heart pounded even harder at Elder Harris's words. She wondered if Matt had recognized the missionary's clever response. He was trying to protect them and the Olsens. He wanted the officer to believe that he was the only missionary left in the house.

The officer's footsteps moved closer to the trunks. Then he kicked one of them with a loud bang.

"Open it!" he demanded.

The children heard the jingle of keys as Elder Harris unlocked the trunk. The lid creaked. Silence followed. Emily and Matt barely dared to breath. Then there was another bang as the officer's foot kicked the next trunk.

"Now this one!" he said.

The second lid creaked open. Matt and Emily huddled next to each other in the third trunk. They each knew that their trunk was next. They had no papers for the officer and no believable excuse for being in Germany. Their only hope was to rely on the Lord. Silently, they kept on praying.

All at once, they heard a new sound. A faint, sweet voice.

"Elder Harris? Elder Harris?"

Matt licked the sweat off his upper lip. He was still alive. He was sure of it. He was still way too uncomfortable to have died. But if he wasn't hearing an angel, who was he hearing?

The voice came again. "Elder Harris? Are you there?"

"Who is that?" The Gestapo officer asked.

"Sister Schmidt," Elder Harris replied. "This is her home. She is the lady who I came to visit. She has been very ill."

There was a moment's silence. When the officer spoke again, his voice was muffled. "Take me to her!" he said.

"You are very smart to cover your face with a handkerchief, officer," Elder Harris said. "Sister Schmidt tells me her illness is life threatening and very contagious. I did not have your wisdom when I was at her bedside."

Elder Harris sighed. "Perhaps I've already contracted the disease myself."

"She is that bad?" The muffled voice behind the handkerchief sounded startled.

"Oh, yes!" Elder Harris said. "Terrible rashes, fevers, hallucinations. It shouldn't be long now."

"Shouldn't be long?" the officer asked. He took a couple of steps backward. "Shouldn't be long until she dies, you mean?"

"Yes." Elder Harris lowered his voice to a whisper. "But no one has told her so. She imagines she is young again and has no thought of dying. Hallucinations, you understand."

"I see," the officer said. "We will leave this house now. You will accompany me to Gestapo headquarters. My superior officer will want to look at your papers."

"But Sister Schmidt . . ." Elder Harris began.

"If the lady of the house is to die, she will die," the officer said, coldly. "You do not need to be here." His feet clicked across the tile toward the door. "And neither do I."

Elder Harris said nothing, but the children heard his softer footsteps move toward the door. The door opened and closed again with a solid thud. Then there was silence.

CHAPTER 7

Matt couldn't stand the heat any longer. Gingerly, he lifted one hand upward until it touched the lid of the trunk. He pushed the lid slowly. A tiny slit of light appeared along the upper edge of the trunk, and some cool, fresh air seeped in.

Matt held the lid steady for a few seconds then pushed it up a little farther. This time the lid gave a high-pitched creak. Matt froze. His hand on the lid trembled as he tried to hold it steady. He held his breath, desperately listening for the sound of footsteps outside the door again, or the shout of a hidden Gestapo officer. No sound came.

He let his breath out slowly. Then he tried gently pushing upward again.

Another squeak.

Another pause.

Matt felt Emily stir behind him, and he squirmed forward, putting his mouth to the wide crack he'd created. Taking a deep gulp of air, he heard Emily doing the same thing. But there was still no other sound.

"D'you think we're okay?" he whispered into the dark space beside him.

Emily was silent for a second. "It feels all right," she finally said, and Matt knew what she meant. They had to rely on the Spirit to guide them.

With a prayer in his heart, Matt plucked up the courage to push the lid open all the way. Sunlight streamed in.

Both he and Emily covered their eyes. Then, when they'd adjusted to the brightness of the entryway, they looked around.

The small room was just as it had been before the arrival of the Gestapo officer.

The children sat up in the trunk, stretching their cramped muscles.

Emily picked up a white shirt that lay beneath her knee and used it to wipe her face. Her ponytail lay limp across her back, and small wisps of hair around her forehead were damp and curly.

Matt had a bright pink circle on his cheek where he'd been pressed up against a book in the trunk. His short, blond hair was sticking out in all directions. He tried flattening it with his hand, but it didn't help much. Even his mom couldn't ever get it to lie down completely.

"What do we do now?" Emily asked, a small quiver in her voice.

"We've got to find the Olsens. They should still be here somewhere," Matt said as he climbed out of the trunk.

He led the way up the steep flight of wooden stairs.

Their first few steps were wobbly, but by the time they reached the upstairs landing, their legs were feeling far more normal.

Old wallpaper with large, faded pink roses covered the wall, and a single lightbulb at the end of a long cord hung from the ceiling.

The children paused on the landing. Three doors faced them; one was ajar.

"Sister Schmidt?" Matt whispered. He moved closer to the door. "Sister Schmidt? Are you in there?"

"Who is it?" came a weak voice from within the room.

Matt gently pushed the door open and stepped in. Emily followed close behind.

An old wooden bed took up most of the space in the small room. Lying in the center of the bed was a frail, elderly lady with snowy white hair. Her thin, gnarled fingers clenched the top of a brown, woolen blanket. Even though the room was warm, she was shivering. Her blue eyes were full of fear.

"Who are you?" Her voice was little more than a croak.

Emily spoke first. "It's all right, Sister Schmidt. The Gestapo officer has gone. I'm Emily Williams, and this is my brother, Matt. We're missionaries. We're trying to find the Olsens."

Before Sister Schmidt could reply, a door to the children's right creaked open. Both Emily and Matt jumped. They turned to see Brother Olsen emerging from within a large wooden closet standing against the bedroom wall. He pushed aside some hanging clothes and reached back inside to guide out a short, elderly lady. She had pearl-gray hair pulled into a small bun on the top of her head. Her face was pale.

"I have rarely been as glad to hear anything as I was to hear your voice, Sister Williams," Elder Olsen said.

He led his wife toward them and introduced her to the children. Then he walked over to the bed and took Sister Schmidt's hand.

"These are friends who have come to help us, Sister Schmidt," he said.

Sister Schmidt's face relaxed into a smile, and she nodded weakly. "That is good," she said. "That is good." Then her eyelids fluttered, and she closed her eyes.

"Come, children," Sister Olsen said softly, pointing to the door. "We need to hear what has happened, but we must let Sister Schmidt rest. Is Elder Harris downstairs?"

"Elder Harris is gone," Matt said.

Elder and Sister Olsen stopped in their tracks. "Gone?" Elder Olsen repeated.

"He left with the Gestapo officer," Emily said.

Sister Olsen gasped and covered her mouth with her hand.

Elder Olsen put an arm around each of the children. "We will go downstairs, and you must tell us everything."

CHAPTER 8

They gathered in the small kitchen. The room was cold, and apart from a chipped mug sitting beside a large, rectangular sink, it looked as though it had gone unused for a long time. Sister Olsen hurried over to the cupboards and opened them one by one until she found a saucepan. This she quickly filled with water from the sink and set on top of the stove in the corner of the room.

The stove was unlike anything the children had seen before. One wide hot plate covered most of the top, and two heavy metal doors opened up in the front. A copper bucket sat beside the left door, with a handful of coal pieces and a small shovel inside. Elder Olsen scooped up a couple lumps of coal, opened the left-hand door, and threw them inside. Then he added a few twisted pieces of newspaper from a nearby shelf and lit them with matches that were beside the newspaper.

The paper caught light immediately. Elder Olsen watched the paper curl and crumble around the waiting coal. Then he closed the door gently, sighed, and pulled himself upright again. "We mustn't waste one lump of Sister Schmidt's coal."

Sister Olsen nodded. "I know dear, but it will be easier to leave if I know Sister Schmidt is warm in her bed. She has such a dreadful chill."

Matt wondered how Sister Schmidt would benefit from two lumps of coal in the kitchen. Emily caught his eye and gave a brief shrug. She'd obviously been wondering the same thing.

Elder Olsen sat at the kitchen table and indicated that the children do the same.

"Now, children," he said, "while Sister Olsen sees to the hot water, I want you to tell me everything that happened between Elder Harris and the Gestapo officer."

It did not take long for Emily and Matt to explain all they'd heard from inside the trunk. The older missionary, in turn, told the children that as soon as he'd realized that a Gestapo officer was at the door, he and his wife had hidden inside the closet upstairs. With the closet door closed, they'd heard nothing until the children arrived in the bedroom.

When the two accounts were told, everyone sat in silence for a few seconds. It was Elder Olsen who finally spoke.

"Well," he said, taking a deep breath, "I believe we should leave here as quickly as possible. Somehow we must find Elder Harris and join Elder Blanchard before the last train comes through town."

He looked over at his wife, who was still standing beside the stove. "Come, my dear," he said, holding out his hand to her. "Before we do anything else, let's pray."

Sister Olsen joined them at the table. They all knelt down on the hard, dark brown tile and bowed their heads. Elder Olsen said the prayer. He prayed for their safety and the safety of Elder Harris. He prayed for help in finding the missing missionary and reaching the railway station in time. As he closed the prayer, Elder Olsen prayed for the blessing of comfort to be with each of them.

The pan on the stove was just beginning to hiss when they rose to their feet. Sister Olsen gave each of the children a hug then returned to the stove. Matt and Emily watched as she lifted down a large metal bottle and a gray woolen cloth from a cupboard above the stove. Carefully, she poured the steaming, boiling water into the bottle and screwed the metal lid on tight. Then she picked up the cloth. As she held it up, the children could see that it had been sewn into the shape of a large pocket. Sister Olsen slid the open end of the pocket over the bottle and soon had the bottle completely wrapped in the gray woolen fabric.

"There," she said, lifting the mysterious gray bundle. "As soon as I've given this to Sister Schmidt, we'll go."

Matt couldn't contain his curiosity any longer. "What is that?"

Sister Olsen looked surprised. "Why, it's a hot water bottle."

"A hot water bottle?"

"Yes, dear. I'll place this in Sister Schmidt's bed beside her feet, and it will keep her warm for a little while."

Elder Olsen stepped forward. "Would you like me to carry it upstairs for you?"

Sister Olsen's pale blue eyes filled with tears. "No, thank you. I need to say good-bye to my friend."

Elder Olsen nodded. "I understand. But, remember, we don't have much time."

Matt, Emily, and Elder Olsen were waiting in the entryway beside the trunks when Sister Olsen returned just a few minutes later. She was wiping tears from her eyes with a handkerchief.

"Sister Schmidt is still very weak, but she is brave. She wants us to go," she said.

Elder Olsen put his arm around her. "Heavenly Father will watch over her. We must put our faith in Him and follow our mission president's instructions."

She nodded and looked over at the trunks.

"We're leaving the trunks?" she said.

"I think we'll have to," Elder Olsen replied, and he bent over to lock the one closest to him.

Matt quickly did the same with the other two.

He was just stepping around the second trunk when a light knock sounded on the door.

Everyone froze.

The knock came again—slightly louder this time.

Matt swallowed hard. There was no time to hide.

Elder Olsen stepped hesitantly toward the door. He had almost reached the handle when they heard a voice outside.

"It's me . . . Otto! Open the door!"

Elder Olsen had the door open almost immediately, and like a shadow, Otto slipped inside. But this time, Otto was not alone.

A pretty lady wearing a faded yellow dress followed close behind him. Her hair was pulled back into a ponytail and was the same blond color as Otto's hair.

"I have brought my mother," Otto announced. "She has come to help Sister Schmidt so that you may leave."

Sister Olsen was the first to overcome her surprise at the news.

"Greta," she said, walking over to Otto's mother and giving her a hug. "How good to see you looking so much better."

Otto's mother smiled. "A few weeks ago, when I was very ill, you took care of me and Otto. Now I must return your kindness. Otto has told me that you must go. I will stay with Sister Schmidt until she is well again."

"Thank you, Greta," Elder Olsen said.

"And I have the cart outside," Otto announced. "For your trunks."

"Way to go, Otto!" Matt said. "Let's get it loaded up."

"Just a minute." Elder Olsen placed his hand on Otto's shoulder. "Before you do that, Otto, can you tell me if you know where the Gestapo headquarters is?"

Emily saw Otto's mother's face go pale.

Otto glanced at his mother, then back at Elder Olsen. "Yes," he said solemnly. "I know where it is."

"Could you take us there?" Elder Olsen asked. "A Gestapo officer has taken Elder Harris away for questioning, and we must do what we can to help him."

Again Otto glanced at his mother. She was looking at him with pain-filled eyes.

"Mother?" he asked softly.

Slowly, she nodded her head. "Yes, Otto. You may go." She reached forward, grasped her son's hand, and looked right into his eyes. "But you must promise me that you will not go inside that building. You may show the missionaries where to find Elder Harris, but you will not go with them if they enter."

"Yes, Mother," Otto said. "I will be careful. And I will come back."

Elder Olsen tenderly put his arm around Otto's mother. "Greta, I'm sorry. I was not thinking."

A single tear ran down her cheek. "Otto will help you," she said. "But I cannot allow him to risk his life."

Emily and Matt looked over at Otto in alarm.

Otto smiled weakly. "Several weeks ago my father was arrested by the Gestapo for writing an article in our local newspaper about our Jewish friends," he explained in a low voice.

"Without warning, the Gestapo entered our friends' home. The officers stole anything of value—everything else was destroyed. They took the father and boys away in one truck, the mother and girls in another. My father saw it happen, but he could not prevent it. He wanted to warn others, and he was careful to write only the truth, but those same Gestapo officers arrived at our home the day the article was printed. My father was taken away."

Otto swallowed hard. "We have not seen or heard from him since."

Matt and Emily stared at him in shocked silence. They tried to imagine how they would feel if their father were suddenly taken away for writing a newspaper article. And even worse than that, they wondered what it would be like to never see him again—not to even know if he were still alive.

Emily licked her dry lips. She tried not to let her growing fear of the Gestapo officers overcome the peaceful feeling she'd felt after Elder Olsen's prayer in the kitchen. Heavenly Father would help them. She had to hold tight to that thought and not let it go.

Without a word, the small group moved closer to the door. Otto cracked it open, peered up and down the street outside, then pushed it wide open. With Matt on one end of a trunk and Otto on the other, the boys piled each one onto the cart.

Elder Olsen took Sister Olsen by the hand and led her out of the house. Emily followed as the two boys each lifted a handle and pushed the cart onto the road. Otto's mother stood at the door, one hand holding the doorknob, the other raised to wave at them. With sadness, the missionaries each waved back, then they turned to make their way down the road as quickly and quietly as they could.

CHAPTER 9

They had only gone a few yards when Matt came to an abrupt halt. "Wait!" he said. "Just one minute."

Then he turned and ran back to the house. Otto's mother was still at the door. When he reached her, he stopped and put his hand into his pocket. He pulled out one of the coins Elder Blanchard had given him.

"Take this," Matt said, handing her the coin. "Use it to buy food for yourself and Sister Schmidt."

Otto's mother gave him a gentle smile. "Thank you," she said. Then she pointed down the alley at the waiting missionaries. "Now go. Go quickly."

Matt nodded and ran back to join the waiting group. Without a word, he raised the baggage cart handle again, and they were on their way.

They walked quickly without talking. Matt and Emily could feel the tension in the air. Innocent things were suddenly frightening. The unexpected flutter of a curtain in a window, the stealthy movement of a cat beside a wall, a distant shout, or the sudden flight of a bird would make Matt and Emily jump. Sometimes they even had the prickly feeling that they were being watched.

The baggage cart was heavy and cumbersome, but Matt and Otto pushed together and shared the weight evenly. Emily watched the road ahead for bumps, ruts, or stones that the boys could not see because of their load.

Elder Olsen held his wife's arm. They walked behind the cart, and even though Elder Olsen limped, it was Sister Olsen who struggled to keep up with the rapid pace set by the children. Her breath was coming out in ragged gasps by the time they at last turned onto a street that they recognized.

It was the road the children had taken from the railway station. The red and black flags again floated above them. The same gray buildings stared down at them with cold, watchful eyes.

"We are very near Gestapo head-quarters now," Otto said, breaking the silence.

"We're close to the railway station too, aren't we?" Emily asked.

"Yes," Otto replied. "We will pass that first." He turned to face Elder Olsen. "We can unload the trunks at the station entrance. Sister Olsen can rest there while you find the other missionaries. I will take Matt and Emily and show them the building that houses Gestapo headquarters."

"Thank you, Otto," Elder Olsen said. He looked worried for his wife. "A few more yards, dear, then you can rest."

Sister Olsen managed a weak smile. "I'll be fine," she gasped, then she coughed hard into her handkerchief. Once her coughing attack subsided, she asked apologetically, "Maybe we could walk this last part a little slower?"

They moved off again, and despite their slower pace, they were soon within sight of the railway station entrance.

"Almost there, my dear," Elder Olsen said.

She bravely walked onward, fighting hard for every breath.

They joined the crowd entering the station. People and their luggage were still everywhere.

The boys pushed forward until Matt spotted a small area next to a wall that was big enough to deposit the trunks. Quickly, they unloaded the cart.

Elder Olsen led Sister Olsen over to the first trunk and sat her down upon it carefully. The others stood beside her, watching anxiously as she struggled to catch her breath.

After a few minutes she raised her head. "Go, children," she urged in a croaky voice. "We don't have much time. We must find Elder Harris. Otto, hurry home to your mother." She reached out her hand and touched Otto's face. "Bless you, child," she gasped. Then her coughing began again.

Elder Olsen knelt down at her side. "I'll stay with Sister Olsen," he told the children. "Go quickly, but be very careful. We should have Elder Blanchard's help by the time you get back."

Otto wheeled the empty cart around and led the way out of the station once more. Before long, all sounds from the railway station were lost to them. Their footsteps echoed eerily off the sidewalk. Several times Matt and Emily turned around, sure that other footsteps were following—but they saw no one.

Otto's eyes darted back and forth, checking doorways and windows for any sign of life. The solid, gray walls and dusty glass panes towered above them. The only obvious movement on the quiet street was the occasional ripple of one of the red and black flags.

As the corner of the road drew near, Otto's footsteps slowed.

"That is their headquarters," he whispered, pointing to an imposing building at the end of the street. Two black cars were parked outside the main doors, but no one was to be seen outside. "We'll walk right past, turn the corner, and find somewhere to hide my cart."

Emily stared at the cart, willing herself not to look up at the Gestapo headquarters as they walked by. Matt glanced briefly up the stone stairs that led to the main entrance. The doors were solid wood with large brass door rings instead of handles. His heart sank. There was no way they could sneak through those doors.

Otto turned the corner. Matt and Emily followed.

The windows on this side of the building were smaller and placed higher in the wall. Heavy wire fencing covered each window pane, giving the building the appearance of a wild animal cage.

The children walked the length of the building until they reached a narrow alley that ran along the back side. Half a dozen metal garbage cans lined the alley. The sour smell of rotting food filled the air.

Matt wrinkled up his nose. "Whew! What a smell!"

A couple of cats, startled by Matt's voice, jumped off the top of a garbage can and streaked past the children and across the street.

The children watched the cats enter an abandoned warehouse on the other side of the road.

"This place seems so empty and sad," Emily said in a quiet voice.

Otto nodded. "Yes, but it didn't used to be like this. It's strange, even for me, to see these buildings so quiet." He pointed to the neglected warehouse. "Farmers used to send their crops to that warehouse. Workers then sent the fruits and vegetables on to all the shops in the city. Now the workers have been sent off to join the army, and the farmers are forced to supply the soldiers with food. Hardly anything reaches the city anymore. We have no need of a warehouse. We barely have need of the shops. There is little to sell and little to buy. You saw that yourselves."

Matt gazed at the empty building. "I bet we could use the warehouse right now. It would be a great place to hide your cart."

"Or hide ourselves!" Emily added. She was starting to worry again.

"It doesn't look like the main door's all the way closed," Matt said. "Let's see if we can get in."

He was right. Within minutes the children had hidden the cart behind the broken warehouse door, and they were back in the alley next to the garbage cans.

"Do we have to stand right here?" Matt wailed, with his fingers pinching his nose tight.

"Shhh!" Otto and Emily said together. But as Otto began to speak again, Emily grabbed his arm and raised her finger to her lips.

"Listen!" she said. "Can you hear it?"

The boys stood quietly. Tensely, Emily motioned for them to follow her, and she walked back along the side of the Gestapo headquarters building until she stood directly below one of the tiny windows. Here, she stopped, cocked her head to one side, and listened intently.

"Can you hear it?" she whispered again to the boys, her eyes shining with excitement.

"'Do What Is Right'!" Matt breathed. "Someone's whistling 'Do What Is Right'!"

"Elder Harris," Otto said, looking up at the window high above. "He's in there!"

Emily followed Otto's gaze. "Yes," she said. "But how do we get him out?"

CHAPTER 10

The three children huddled against the wall and prayed. They knew that they could not free Elder Harris alone.

A stray dog wandered across the road and sniffed their legs with interest. Otto reached down and absently stroked its head. Then he paused, wrapped his hands around the animal's thin body, and lifted it up.

"I wonder," he said slowly, looking at the dog more carefully. "How would you like to play in a huge pile of stinky garbage, boy?" he asked. "And we will even add some alley cats to the bargain."

Matt and Emily looked at him blankly, and Otto's smile broadened. "I promised my mother that I would not enter Gestapo headquarters," he said. "So you will have to rescue Elder Harris without me. You know where he's being held. You have only to get inside the building and past the guards."

"Oh, sure!" Emily said. "Only get inside and past the guards! Nothing to it!"

"Well, all right, it may not be easy," Otto admitted, "but you will not be totally without help. We have prayed. And now we have a new friend."

Otto petted the dog's head, and the dog leaned forward to lick Otto's chin. "The dog and I will give you three minutes to get near the main doors.

Then we are going to knock over cans, chase cats, chew up garbage, and make an awful lot of noise here in the alley. If we are lucky, those suspicious guards will come running to find out what is happening. The dog and I will be chased one way, while you and Elder Harris escape in the other direction."

Matt and Emily could only stare. It was daring. It was completely nuts. But it was probably the only chance they had. Matt dug his hand into his pocket and pulled out a small coin. He gave the German mark to Otto.

"You deserve a lot more," he said. "I'll never forget you."

Otto took the coin and slipped it into his own pocket with a grin. "Just remember, I will be up to my knees in that awful garbage. I may not be able to stand the smell for long. Work fast!"

"Thanks, Otto," Emily said. "And good luck!"

"Good luck to you too," he said with a quick wave. "Remember, three minutes!"

It all happened too fast. Otto and the dog were gone, hidden in the alley. Matt and Emily ran to the corner of the building, checked that no one was on guard outside the main doors, then sidled over to the stairs. A heavy stone railing ran up the stairs and hung over the sidewalk by just a few inches. Matt and Emily bent low beneath it and hugged the wall beside the stairs, silently praying that they would not be seen from above. Then they counted thirty-six tense seconds until an incredible clanging and barking and meowing filled the air.

Within seconds, the solid doors above them burst open and the sound of heavy, booted feet pounded down the stairs.

Matt and Emily waited until the five men turned the corner of the building, then they bolted up the stairs and into the lobby of the Gestapo headquarters.

Barely pausing to catch their breath, the children ran down a hallway that led off to the left. A thick red carpet hid the sound of their running feet as they followed the hallway past several closed doors.

"How much farther, do you think?" Emily panted.

"I don't know," Matt replied, slowing his feet. "It seemed like the whistling came from about three-quarters of the way down this side of the building—but there are so many doors in here!"

Emily stopped and looked up and down the hall. "We'll have to pick one," she said desperately. "And just keep trying till we get it right."

"Okay," Matt agreed. He pointed to the closest door. "That one!"

Before either of them could think through the consequences, he grasped the door handle and pushed open the door. They tumbled inside, closed the door behind them, and leaned back against it.

They had entered an office—and someone had been there very recently. A burning cigarette lay in an ashtray on the desk, filling the room with hazy smoke. A half-full cup of coffee sat beside it.

Emily rushed over to the small window and peered outside.

"We're not far enough back yet," she said, judging their position by the warehouse across the road. "Come on! Quick!"

Matt's hand was already on the doorknob when they heard voices coming down the hall.

Emily grabbed his arm and dragged him back to the desk.

Without a word, they both dived underneath it and crouched low as the door to the office opened.

"Are they all still outside?" an angry voice shouted. "How many of them does it take to sort out a catfight?"

"I don't know, sir," came a second voice. "Perhaps there was more to it than just a few cats."

"Why I can't ever be sent officers of any intelligence, I'll never know! I will have to see to it myself!"

There was a loud jingle and thud as something heavy was dropped onto the desk, followed by the rustle of papers and the whisper of footsteps across the thick carpet.

"Has that idiot American stopped singing yet?" the first man asked.

"Yes, sir," said the second man. "But he's started whistling now. We've moved him to the very end of the hall so he won't disturb you."

There was a grunt of approval. "He'll be on the first truck out of here tonight," the first man said, and the door closed with a solid click.

Matt and Emily crawled out from under the desk without a word. More scared than they'd ever been before, they stood up and faced the door together.

Emily glanced down at the desk and gasped. She reached down and picked up a small blue book and a handful of papers. She stuffed them into her pocket and snatched the large ring of keys that the officer had dropped onto the desk.

"Come on!" Matt urged from the door. "He's in the one at the end of the hall."

Matt opened the door a crack and put his ear to it. With a brief nod to Emily, he opened it completely, and they slipped out.

Emily shut the door behind them and sprinted after her brother to the end of the hall.

They could hear Elder Harris still whistling behind the door.

Matt grabbed the key ring from Emily's outstretched hand and tried one of the keys in the lock. It went into the keyhole, but wouldn't turn.

He jiggled it. It still wouldn't unlock the door.

"Hurry, Matt! Hurry!" Emily whispered.

"I'm doing my best. You just keep your eyes on the hallway."

Matt pulled the key out and tried a second one. It didn't fit.

He fumbled with the key ring and tried another. It was too small.

Emily kept glancing over her shoulder to check the hall. "Come on, Matt!"

With shaking hands, Matt tried a fourth key.

It slid into the hole and turned. Finally, the door opened, and he burst into the room.

Elder Harris was sitting on a cement floor in a completely empty room. One side of his face was purple and swollen. His glasses were bent, the lenses cracked. It was taking every bit of his strength to pucker his swollen lips and blow out a tune. He raised his head as the door flew open and stopped whistling mid-note.

"Brother and Sister Williams?" he gasped, staggering to his feet.

"No time to explain," Matt said, seizing the missionary's sleeve. "We've got to get out of here."

Elder Harris didn't need to be told twice. He stumbled out of the small room.

Emily threw the keys onto the floor and closed the door on them.

They raced down the hall and had almost reached the lobby when the sound of voices and footsteps on the stone stairs outside reached them.

"They're coming back!" gasped Emily. "We've got to hide."

Matt reached for the closest doorknob. "It's locked," he said, frantically trying to turn it. "Try the next door!"

Emily was there first.

She tried turning the knob. "This one's locked too!" she cried.

Elder Harris was already trying a third door—but it wouldn't budge.

"Which one were we in before?" Matt asked.

Emily chewed her lower lip and scanned the row of doors. "I don't know! That one, maybe?" she said, pointing down the hall and starting to run back that way.

Matt and Elder Harris were right behind her when another loud voice reached them from the street outside.

"Commandant, sir! I believe the men have found something!"

The sound of the footsteps entering the lobby stopped suddenly.

"What do you mean, 'found something,' sergeant?"

The children recognized the man's voice from earlier in the office. He sounded angry and impatient.

"I don't know, sir." The other man outside sounded uneasy. "The men in the alley respectfully request your presence."

"I am surrounded by men who can't do anything without a commanding officer present!"

The children heard the commandant's footsteps begin again—this time headed outside.

"It had better be worth my time, sergeant!"

The footsteps continued down the stairs. Elder Harris, Matt, and Emily looked at each other.

"Now!" Elder Harris hissed. "It's our only chance before they're all back in the building."

They dashed all the way to the front lobby, but slowed their steps as they reached the door.

They were almost there when Matt caught a movement out of the corner of his eye. He turned and saw another Gestapo officer approaching them from the hallway on the opposite side of the building. Matt gave his sister a warning poke in the ribs and cleared his throat nervously.

Elder Harris looked up, then he immediately turned his head, hiding the bruises on his face from the approaching officer.

The officer looked at them questioningly. Emily forced a smile.

"We . . . uh . . . we were wondering what was going on outside," she said, before the officer could say a word. "Did you hear all the noise too?"

The officer's mouth formed a grim, straight line. "I've never witnessed such chaos! There's been more confusion in this building in one day than I've seen in six months at my office in Berlin."

"Well, I think the commandant has gone out to check on it," Emily said, bravely facing the officer as though she had nothing else to worry about.

"Has he indeed?" The officer looked interested. "Well, maybe I can be of assistance to him. If you'll excuse me." He brushed by with his head held high.

Elder Harris, Matt, and Emily waited only until he'd reached the corner of the building, then they bolted down the stairs and ran along the street heading away from the alley, the warehouse, and the Gestapo.

"Em, you were awesome!" Matt panted as they ran.

"I'm surprised he didn't hear my knees knocking," she panted back.

"He was too full of himself to notice anything as puny as your knees," Matt countered.

Elder Harris gave a lopsided grin. His face was still swelling. "You were both brilliant," he said. "I can't believe you just busted me out of Gestapo headquarters!"

"Yeah!" crowed Matt.

"We're not free and clear yet," Emily quickly reminded him, with an anxious look over her shoulder. "And I sure hope Otto got away."

Matt was serious again. "We couldn't have done it without Otto," he told Elder Harris. "He was the one in the alley making all that noise."

Elder Harris looked concerned. "Well, as Emily said, none of us are safe yet, so let's keep on praying—for all the missionaries and for Otto."

CHAPTER 11

Once they'd put a little distance between themselves and Gestapo head-quarters, Elder Harris, Matt, and Emily slowed their pace. They darted in and out of building entryways, hiding behind stairs and walls as they worked their way up the street. They were standing together in the doorway of an apartment building when they heard three gunshots fired, one right after the other.

"Otto!" Emily screamed.

Elder Harris immediately clapped one hand over her mouth and used his other arm to hold her close. Emily buried her face in his coat and cried. For several minutes they stood, huddled together, not saying a word.

Emily heard Matt sniffing beside her, but by the time she raised her red-rimmed eyes, he was looking back down the street toward the Gestapo headquarters with an expression of quiet determination on his face.

Elder Harris used his hand to wipe the tears off Emily's face. "We must go," he said grimly.

Matt stepped out onto the sidewalk and began walking back the way they'd come.

"No," Elder Harris said, reaching out to grab Matt's arm. "Not that way."

"But we can't just leave Otto. He risked his life for us!" Matt said, his voice shaking.

Elder Harris dropped his arm. "Exactly. And that's why we mustn't go back. If we return to that awful place and get caught, everything Otto did was for nothing. But if we keep going, we can still make it to the station by eleven thirty—and that's what Otto would want us to do."

The missionary pushed his loose, broken glasses back onto the bridge of his nose. Behind the cracked lenses, Emily could see the sadness in Elder Harris's eyes. This was as hard for him as it was for them.

"He's right, Matt," Emily said softly.

Matt looked at her bleakly then hung his head. "I know."

Elder Harris put an arm around Matt's shoulders. "Come on. Let's go and find Elder Blanchard."

They had no time to waste. Trying desperately to keep their hope and faith alive, the children focused on what they had been asked to do. Once again, they turned to face their destination and stepped out from the shadow of the doorway.

Glancing back often, they saw some of the Gestapo officers returning to their building. It was hard not to take off running, but they knew that it would attract attention. So they continued on at a brisk walk, each silently praying for Otto and that no one would think to check on the American prisoner.

They were about halfway to the station when they heard the faint but unmistakable sound of a train whistle carried on the light breeze.

"It's coming!" Matt cried.

They started to run, but so did many other people, who all converged on the station from different directions. The growing crowd pressed forward through the large iron gates of the station and toward the platform. They were being carried away by the movement around them, but Matt wiggled free.

"This way," he called, pulling on Elder Harris's coat sleeve and trusting that his sister would follow. "We left the Olsens over here."

They fought their way against the tide of people until they reached the spot where Matt and Otto had unloaded the trunks. But there was no sign of the missionaries—or their luggage. They stood close together, scouring the crowd for a familiar face.

"What if they've left us?" Emily said, her heart sinking. "What if they're already on the train?"

"Why don't you try whistling?" said a voice from behind them.

Elder Harris, Matt, and Emily swung around.

"Otto!" Matt and Emily gasped together. "Otto, you're alive!"

Giddy with relief and happiness, Matt threw his arms around his friend. "We heard the shots. We thought . . . how did you . . ."

Otto held up a hand. "There is no time for questions. Whistle. Whistle now for Elder Blanchard." He pushed his cart toward them. "Stand on this, Matt, and whistle as loud as you can!"

Matt looked over at Elder Harris.

The missionary gently touched his even more swollen face. "It's up to you, my friend. I don't think I'm able to whistle anymore."

Without another word, Matt climbed up onto Otto's cart.

He puckered up his lips and began to whistle, "Do what is right; the day-dawn is breaking . . ." It was faint at first, but gradually swelled in volume, until those around him were all turning to stare.

Suddenly a man in a dark gray overcoat pushed his way through the crowd, reached out, and grabbed Matt by the shirt.

He gazed at the missionary name tag then pulled Matt toward him. With his cold, dark eyes never leaving Matt's face, the man spoke in harsh, rapid German.

"What do you think you are doing?"

Otto studied the man's uniform, barely visible beneath the gray coat. He cupped his hand over his mouth and whispered to Emily, "Police!"

Emily took a deep breath. Was that better than the Gestapo or worse? She didn't know.

"I repeat," the man growled, his face only inches from Matt's, "what do you think you are doing?"

Matt swallowed hard. "Whistling," he answered. But as soon as he'd said the words, he realized that he'd spoken in English

The man's grip tightened. "You are American," he hissed. "Why are you here?"

"We're . . . we're missionaries," Matt squeaked.

"Missionaries?" the tall man sneered, looking from Matt to Emily and back. "You are children. Children cannot be missionaries."

"Children can be the best missionaries," challenged another voice.

Elder Blanchard stepped up out of the crowd.

"These children are with me. We're missionaries for The Church of Jesus Christ of Latter-day Saints," he said.

The policeman glared at Elder Blanchard. "Your name?" he demanded, taking a step forward and pushing Matt to one side.

Emily moved over to stand beside her brother. They exchanged frightened looks, but they didn't dare say a word.

"Thomas Blanchard," the missionary replied in a clear voice.

He took off his hat. His dark hair lay smooth and tidy, except for a faint ridge that circled his head. Matt put a hand to his own hair. It had never recovered from his time in the trunk, but it probably wasn't much messier than usual. Somehow it was comforting to know that even great missionaries, like Elder Blanchard, had problems with their hair.

It did nothing to distract from Elder Blanchard's presence, however. He was tall enough to look the officer in the eye, and if he was nervous, he didn't show it.

"Papers," the officer said, holding out his hand.

Elder Blanchard reached into his jacket pocket and brought out a passport, along with an assortment of other pieces of paper. He handed them over.

Emily stiffened. Trying hard not to make a sound, she slipped her hand into the pocket of her jeans. She eased out the small blue book and papers that she'd taken from the desk at Gestapo headquarters. Without a word she passed them to Elder Harris.

He took them from her just as quietly and glanced down at them. His eyes widened, then his shoulders relaxed with relief.

"Thank you," he mouthed silently.

She smiled then turned her attention back to the police officer. He was flipping through the pages of Elder Blanchard's passport, barely looking at it.

"Why was this boy standing on the cart whistling?" he finally asked.

"He knew I was waiting here for him. I have tickets for these missionaries, and he was trying to find me in the crowd," Elder Blanchard said.

"And you?" The officer turned to Elder Harris. "What happened to your face?"

Elder Harris didn't flinch. "Someone hit me," he said.

"You've been fighting?"

"No, sir. I didn't hit back."

The police officer looked at the missionary scornfully, but whatever he might have said was drowned out by a piercing whistle and the loud hiss of steam. Matt and Emily watched a large cloud of smoke float skyward. Squealing wheels and shunting pistons signaled that the waiting train was beginning to move. The crowd on the platform still pressed forward, trying hard to reach the train before it sped up. But it didn't slow down enough for anyone to jump on board—and within seconds it was gone.

The children looked at Elder Blanchard in dismay. The officer was also looking at him, a smug expression on his face.

"You have missed the train," he said.

"We will catch the next one," Elder Blanchard said calmly.

"You could have taken this one," the officer pointed out. "Instead you waited for these other missionaries to come and missed your chance to go."

"I couldn't leave without them," Elder Blanchard said. "We'll catch the next one—together."

"There may not be another train for many hours," the officer said. "And you are behind a great crowd of people all wanting to board the same train."

Elder Blanchard shrugged. "I don't know how it will be done, but I do know that the Lord will help us."

For a moment the policeman said nothing. Then he thrust Elder Blanchard's passport back into his hands. "Americans are mad! Missionaries are mad! That makes you doubly mad!"

He faced the small group. "You have until five o'clock to be out of this city; otherwise, you will all accompany me to Gestapo headquarters." He gave a mean smile. "Perhaps your belief in God will be tested enough by then."

Without a backward glance, the policeman marched away toward the quiet street outside the railway station.

"Whoa!" Matt said, sitting down in a heap on the empty baggage cart. "I don't want to go through that again."

"I'm guessing we just saw the nice side of him," Elder Harris said. "It could have gotten a lot uglier if he'd asked for my papers first."

"Do you have them?" Elder Blanchard asked.

"I do now. Sister Williams just gave them to me." Elder Harris looked at Emily with a puzzled expression. "Where did you find them?"

"On the commandant's desk at Gestapo headquarters. When Matt and I were hiding in his office, I saw your name on the papers and grabbed them."

Elder Harris and Elder Blanchard stared at her in amazement.

"It's her eyes," Matt explained. "They may look a little weird, but they work great. She's always catching things other people miss."

Otto and the two missionaries glanced at Emily's eyes.

"Wow!" Elder Harris said.

Otto looked impressed. Emily looked embarrassed. Matt wished he'd been born with one green eye and one blue eye, instead of hair that wouldn't lie flat.

"It sounds like we have a lot to thank you kids for," Elder Blanchard said. "I'd like to hear more about your time at Gestapo headquarters, but first we'd better get moving—just in case that police officer returns."

CHAPTER 12

Elder Blanchard led the way with Elder Harris beside him and the children close behind. They wove through the crowd, walking around piles of luggage and small clusters of people.

The group soon arrived at the far end of the railway station. There, at the edge of the platform, beneath an old lamppost, stood a solitary trunk.

"Hey, that's my trunk!" Elder Harris said, as they approached. "I never thought I'd see it again."

Elder Blanchard placed his hand on Otto's shoulder. "The children brought it to the station on Otto's cart. Elder Wyatt helped me drag it over here with the Olsens' trunks. Elder Wyatt wanted to stay, but I persuaded him to go with the Olsens. Elder Olsen was having a hard time lifting their luggage alone, and Sister Olsen's health isn't good. They left on the train that just pulled out."

Emily smiled. She was surprised by how much this news cheered her. "I'm glad they made it out."

Elder Blanchard sat down on the trunk and made room for Elder Harris beside him. The children sat on the edge of the baggage cart.

"Yes, it was a blessing," Elder Blanchard said with a sigh. "Even with all the challenges and suffering in Germany now, we don't have to look far to see blessings—great and small. We may not always recognize Heavenly Father's help when it's given, but it's there."

"We were helped," Matt said, and he told Elder Blanchard about the rescue of Elder Harris.

"I was helped too," added Otto solemnly when Matt had finished his account.

"How did you get back here?" Emily asked. "And did those men . . . did they shoot at you?"

Otto leaned back against the side of the baggage cart. "No," he said with terrible sadness. "They shot at the dog— and the cats."

Stunned, Matt and Emily listened as Otto explained what had happened.

"When we separated, I ran back to the alley with the dog. Even though he was hidden under my shirt, those alley cats could tell he was there. They were arching their backs and hissing long before I let him out."

Otto smiled as he pictured the scene. "The dog went wild, chasing one cat, then another. The cats were howling and running for their lives, knocking lids off cans and sending them flying against the building. The cans went down. Garbage was everywhere. The dog was having the time of his life— and then the tomcat showed up.

"He had been sleeping under a box, I think, and he was not happy about being woken up—especially by a scruffy stray dog. He climbed up on the wall and leaped onto the dog, digging his claws into the dog's back, spitting, and hissing like a steam engine.

"Then I heard the men coming, and I ran out of there faster than any of the cats—straight across the street into the warehouse. There were a few old crates not far from the door. I climbed inside one of them and waited.

"Within seconds, the men were yelling. It sounded like they were still in the alley so I peeked out through a crack in the wooden wall. The dog had his teeth in the ankle of one officer, and the tomcat was madly scratching another one. The other men were trying so hard to get away from the animals that they were falling over in the garbage.

"I still do not know why the animals decided to turn on the men instead of each other, but I decided I had better leave before the officers could do a thorough search. I was pulling my cart out of its hiding place when they started shooting. The animals ran away, and one of the men started to laugh. It was a cruel, evil laugh. I knew I had to leave fast.

"I thought my heart would thump right out of my chest every time the sound of this old cart's squeaky wheels echoed in that empty warehouse. But I guess the officers were too busy shouting orders at each other to notice anything else. I made it out through the exit at the back. Once I was out, I couldn't go straight home. I had to know if you had found Elder Harris and escaped in time."

"There were so many things that could've gone wrong—that almost did go wrong—for all of us," Emily said quietly. "It was a huge miracle."

Elder Harris looked at the children, his eyes shining. "A miracle that saved my life."

Elder Blanchard put his arm around the other missionary. "I think you've suffered the most through all of this, Elder."

Elder Harris took off his broken glasses and touched his face tenderly. "I'll be okay, thanks to all of you," he said. "One of the Gestapo officers didn't like the answers I gave to his questions. I may not be able to whistle for a while, and I think I'll need to buy new glasses when we get out of here, but that's nothing compared to what could have happened."

Elder Blanchard nodded. "And so we wait together," he said with determination. "We wait for the next train, and we keep on praying—with thanks and with hope and with faith." He turned to Otto. "And you, my fine young friend, must leave us. Your mother will be very worried by now."

Otto stood up. "Yes," he agreed. "I should go."

Matt and Emily stood up too, and Otto picked up the handles of the empty baggage cart. He smiled at Matt and Emily. "Good luck. I hope another train comes very soon."

"Thanks, Otto," Emily said. "Thanks for everything."

Otto grinned. "Not everything," he said. "I think perhaps God helped the most."

Matt and Emily smiled back. "I think you're right," Matt agreed.

Then with a quick wave to the group, Otto swung the baggage cart around and disappeared into the crowd.

CHAPTER 13

The missionaries sat together beside the trunks for over four hours. The afternoon sun beat down on them. Everyone was hot, thirsty, and hungry, but they didn't complain. They were thinking of the people and places they were leaving behind—and the challenges that still lay ahead. Without drawing attention to themselves, they were each silently praying.

When Matt's stomach growled for the third time, Elder Blanchard produced the remains of a small loaf of bread from his pocket. He broke it into four equal pieces and handed one piece to each person.

Even though the bread was dry, it was food, and they accepted it gratefully. But when Emily tried eating her piece, her teeth ground against something hard. She put her fingers in her mouth and pulled out three splinters of wood. Elder Blanchard saw her stare at the slivers in her hand.

"I'm sorry," he said. "Good food is hard to find in Germany right now. Sometimes, if the baker runs short of flour, he adds sawdust to his dough."

Matt immediately stopped chewing. With difficulty, he swallowed what was in his mouth and slid the little bread he had left into his pocket. He didn't feel hungry anymore. Emily brushed the wood slivers off her hand without comment.

When four o'clock came and went, it became much harder to wait patiently. Matt found himself checking his watch more and more often. At four thirty he saw Elder Blanchard check his watch too. He watched the missionary scan the crowd, and he knew he was looking for the police officer in the dark gray overcoat.

At four forty-five Matt stood up. He was too nervous to sit any longer. They were only fifteen minutes from the police officer's deadline, and not a single train had arrived at the station.

He looked back at the crowded platform once more—and paused.

Something had changed. People were stirring. A few were on their feet, dragging their bags even closer to the edge of the platform.

"What's happening?" he asked the older missionaries.

Elder Blanchard stood up and looked around. "I don't know," he began, but then he stopped and listened. Floating in on the gentle breeze was the unmistakable chuff-chuff of an approaching train. Others around them heard it too. Suddenly voices became more anxious. People who had been sitting slumped over baggage stood up with renewed energy.

"Quick!" said Elder Blanchard. "Grab the other end of this trunk, Elder Harris."

The missionaries lifted the trunk and dragged it forward. Matt and Emily followed close behind. Eventually they found themselves right at the end of the railway platform. Most of the other people were gathered near the middle.

"If it's a really long train, we have a chance of getting on board," Elder

Harris said. "If it's a short one, we've had it. I reckon we'll need at least ten carriages if they're to reach us on this end."

Elder Blanchard nodded, and they all turned to look down the track. The sound of the train was drawing nearer and nearer, but it still hadn't come into view. Matt glanced over at Emily. Her hands were clasped tightly, and she kept her eyes on the distant train track. She was as nervous as he was.

Finally there was a clear, loud whistle, and a puff of steam appeared above a grove of trees near the bend in the track. Within seconds, the engine came into sight. The chugging, squealing, and hissing became louder and louder. Elder Blanchard leaned toward Matt and Emily.

"Start counting carriages," he shouted above the noise of the train.

As the first carriage appeared around the bend, they began to count.

One . . . two . . .

The children pressed forward, straining to see.

Three . . . four . . .

The train was slowing down.

Seven, eight, nine . . .

Matt gave a whoop. "Ten!" he yelled. "Ten carriages!"

Elder Blanchard grinned.

"Get ready to board," he shouted back.

Emily pointed at the train. "They're still coming," she called. "Look, that's fourteen!"

Sure enough, when the engine finally steamed to a stop, there were fourteen carriages lined up along the platform—and three of the most empty ones were right in front of the missionaries. Elder Blanchard didn't waste a second.

"Get the trunk on board," he shouted to Elder Harris. "Then see if you can find a seat."

Elder Harris rushed forward and heaved the trunk up the carriage steps. Elder Blanchard pushed from below, and Elder Harris dragged it inside.

"Come on, kids," Elder Blanchard yelled as the crowds of people from the center of the platform surged toward them. He jumped onto the bottom step of the carriage and held out his hand for Emily. She grasped it and leaped on board. Matt was right behind her. They stood on the step together and looked back at the mass of people on the platform below them.

Suddenly Emily grabbed Matt's arm. "Matt, look!" she yelled, pointing out above the crowd. "Look at that door."

Matt's gaze followed the direction of Emily's arm. Not far from the main entrance to the railway station, he could just make out three very plain wooden doors. But one of those doors had a strange bluish light streaming out through the cracks around the door frame. Matt swung back to face Emily.

"That's it, Em!" he cried. "Come on!"

Matt turned to Elder Blanchard. "We've got to go."

"Go? Go where?" the missionary asked. But Matt and Emily were already back on the station platform.

"Back home," Matt yelled up to him.

"Back the way we came," Emily added.

Elder Blanchard didn't call the children back. Instead, he raised his hand to them. "Thanks for your missionary service, Brother and Sister Williams."

"Good luck!" Matt shouted.

"Bye," Emily called and waved.

A stream of people rushed forward to climb on board, and Elder Blanchard was forced to enter the carriage. Within seconds he was lost from their view.

"Come on, Matt," Emily urged. "We've got to find that door."

Everyone was moving toward the waiting train, but the children were trying to go in the opposite direction. Emily found small gaps between people and squeezed through. Matt stayed close behind her.

After what seemed like hours, they broke free and found themselves at the back of the railway station, not far from the main entrance. As they stopped to catch their breath, the train whistle sounded. Steam hissed. Wheels squealed. Matt and Emily turned to watch the train slowly build up speed and move away from the station.

Matt looked at Emily. "I hope we were right about this," he said.

Emily took a deep breath. "We have to be," she said.

CHAPTER 14

Emily reached for Matt's arm. "Quick!" she said. "The door was over this way."

They hurried forward again, and within seconds Matt gave a cheer.

"I see it!" he cried. "Look!"

Matt pointed at a door in the far corner of the railway station. Emily looked. As before, a pale blue light was glowing brightly around the door frame. Emily's anxious expression was replaced by an excited smile, and without a word the children began running toward the door.

They were within just a few yards of their goal when a loud, commanding voice boomed over the noise of the crowd behind them.

"Halt!"

Instinctively, Matt and Emily swung around.

To their horror, the officer who had met them in the lobby of Gestapo headquarters was standing at the station entrance.

They saw him glance to the left and the right and raise his arm.

"They're here!" he shouted, and suddenly two more Gestapo officers emerged from the crowd.

"Go no farther!" The officer was striding toward the children.

The other two officers were on the move too, working their way quickly through the crowd and approaching Matt and Emily from either side.

Matt looked at Emily. "Em, this is one time when we're not going to be polite. Run for it!"

Emily didn't argue. She took off after her brother just as fast as she could. They heard the officers break into a run behind them. Their hard boots clacked across the wooden floor as they took up the chase.

"Stop those children!" one officer yelled.

Out of the corner of her eye, Emily saw people turn their heads to watch, but no one made a move to help the officers, and the children forged on.

Her breath was coming out in short gasps when disaster struck. A shoelace that had come loose suddenly flopped forward beneath her foot. Emily tripped and fell. She hit the wooden floor with a solid thud and immediately heard Matt's frantic voice.

"Em! Em, are you all right? Get up!" He was back by her side in seconds, reaching down and pulling her by the arm. "Come on, Emily. Hurry!"

Desperately fighting back the tears and trying to ignore the pounding pain in both knees, Emily struggled to her feet. Behind her, she could hear the officers' voices barking orders to people in the crowd, but the people around her were standing shoulder to shoulder in a tight protective wall.

"Go quickly, children," an elderly man whispered urgently. "We will slow them down as best we can, but we cannot hold them back for long."

Emily yanked the loose shoe off her foot. There was no time to tie the lace again.

"Thank you," she murmured, wiping a tear from her cheek. "Thank you so much."

Then, as she stumbled forward with one shoe on and one shoe in her hand, the crowd gently parted, then closed ranks again after she'd passed through.

Seconds later they reached the door.

Breathlessly, Matt grasped the knob, twisted it, and yanked the door open. They tumbled inside and threw themselves back against the door. They could still hear running footsteps outside—getting closer and closer.

"Now what?" Emily cried. "Now what do we do?"

"Quick!" shouted Matt. "Take off your missionary name tag. Put it in the envelope."

With trembling fingers, Emily unpinned her black tag. Matt thrust his tag into her hand. He stayed, leaning against the door, as Emily moved over to pick up the glowing envelope. It lay just where they had left it on the old wooden desk, surrounded by the shovels, rakes, hoes, and sacks.

Emily dropped the missionary tags into the envelope. She slid it back onto the desk and hurried back to Matt's side. Together they leaned against the door. Matt and Emily squeezed their eyes shut and waited fearfully. Suddenly, the officers were banging on the door.

"Open up!"

The doorknob rattled as the bright blue light in the shed began to swirl, and they heard the low-pitched humming sound.

Then there was silence.

No shouts. No muffled sound of the crowd outside. No sound of running feet. Just complete silence.

For a few moments, neither of the children spoke.

"Well?" Matt finally whispered. "What d'you think?"

"I don't hear them anymore," she whispered back.

Matt nodded. He put his ear to the door and listened again.

"D'you think we're home?" he asked when he raised his head.

Emily took a deep breath. "Well, there's only one way to find out," she said and pointed at the doorknob. "Go ahead."

Matt took a small step away from the door.

"Oh no! I don't think so," he said. "You do it!"

Emily stared at Matt, then at the doorknob, then back at Matt again.

"Okay," she finally whispered. "We'll do it together."

Matt gave a small grin. "It's a deal!"

Emily placed her hand on the doorknob and looked up at Matt expectantly. Matt stepped forward. He wiped his right hand down his shirt and placed it over his sister's hand.

"On the count of three," Emily said. "We turn the knob and open the door."

"Okay," Matt agreed, and slowly Emily began counting.

When she said, "Three," they both cranked the doorknob to the right and pulled. The door flew open. Emily fell back into Matt, and they ended up in a heap on the shed floor, looking out through the open door at the grounds of the MTC.

"We're home!" cried Emily with relief.

Matt scrambled to his feet and shut the shed door. "Not yet!" he warned. "We've still got to get back up the tree. Missionaries are coming!"

Emily stayed where she was, sitting on the shed floor, until the voices of the missionaries passed by. After waiting a few minutes, Matt opened the door again. This time he opened it carefully and peeked outside through a small chink. When he was satisfied that the coast was clear, he beckoned to Emily, and they slipped out of the shed.

They hurried around the corner and stood below the wall that separated the MTC from their backyard. Matt eyed the wall critically.

"D'you think you could give me a boost up there?" he asked Emily.

Emily nodded. "Yes," she said, "but then how do I get up?"

"I'll reach down for you," Matt said. "Come on! Someone else could walk by any minute."

"Wait, Matt! Look!" Emily pointed over Matt's shoulder to an object lying against the side of the shed.

It was the soccer-ball. Matt ran over, picked it up, and hurled it over the wall. There was a muffled thud as it hit the grass of their backyard, then Matt was back beside his sister. With a quick look over her shoulder, Emily bent down, cupped her hands, and boosted Matt up the wall until his hands could grasp the top ledge.

"Okay," he grunted. "Hang on a second."

He hoisted himself upward, and with only one "ouch" when he scraped his knee, he was soon lying on top of the wall. He leaned over and extended his arms down to Emily.

"Grab my hands," he said, "and use your feet on the wall."

Matt's pull gave her the extra couple of inches that she needed to reach the top of the wall. Within seconds they were crawling along the ledge, one after the other, toward the ash tree branch that hung over the wall.

CHAPTER 15

At last they were home—in their own backyard.

Matt and Emily sat in the tree gazing down at the shed on the other side of the wall. It looked just like any other garden shed. A robin flew down and landed on the gray tile roof. The strange, pale blue light around the door was gone.

A group of missionaries dressed in white shirts, dark pants, and ties, rounded the corner of a building some distance away.

Matt and Emily watched them walk along the sidewalk, past the shed, and on to another building. Everything seemed so normal.

Emily turned to Matt. "Did we . . . I mean . . . did I just imagine it, or did we . . ."

Matt smiled. He shoved his hand into one of his pockets. When he pulled it out again, his fist was tightly closed. He opened it slowly in front of Emily. Sitting on the palm of his hand was a small coin—the last of the German marks that Elder Blanchard had given him.

"We really did it, Em," Matt said.

Emily looked back over at the shed. "Do you think it could ever happen again? The blue light, the mission call, the name tags?"

Matt shrugged. "I don't know. Maybe. Other people serve lots of missions.

Grandma and Grandpa have been on three already." He grinned at her. "Are you up for it?"

Emily thought about her fear when they found themselves in an unknown country—with the dark buildings, the strange language, the constant threat of being arrested by the Gestapo.

Then she thought of the people— the missionaries, Otto, his mother, and Sister Schmidt. She remembered the prayers, the guidance of the Holy Ghost, the miracles, and the protection they'd received.

"Yes," she said slowly. "Being a missionary is a pretty amazing thing."

Matt nodded, turning the German mark over and over in his hand.

"D'you think they made it out?" he asked at last. "All of them?"

Emily sat quietly for a few seconds, thinking of the wonderful people they'd left behind. "Yes," she said finally. A feeling of peace slowly filled her heart. "I think they did."

Matt smiled. "Me too." He paused, then added, "And I hope we made a difference."

Emily's gaze followed her brother's to the small coin. She remembered where the other German marks had gone—to help Otto and his mother and Sister Schmidt.

"I guess even little things can make a difference," she said.

"Yeah," Matt agreed. Then he looked up with a grin. "Hey! Who're you calling little? I may be your younger brother, but I can beat you down this tree any day!"

With that, Matt shot down the tree and set off across the lawn as fast as a jackrabbit.

"Matt! Wait!" Emily called.

But Matt just laughed and kept on running. Emily leaned back against the tree and groaned.

Things were definitely back to normal.

AUTHOR'S NOTE

Although the adventures of Matt and Emily are fictitious, this story is based upon the inspirational events that occurred during the August 1939 evacuation of LDS missionaries from Germany.

On the morning of Thursday, August 24, 1939, President Hugh B. Brown (then serving as president of the British Mission) contacted the mission home in West Germany. He had been given an important assignment from the First Presidency. With the telephone lines down in Germany, the First Presidency had not been able to reach the missionaries there directly. They had asked President Brown to pass on an urgent message from President Heber J. Grant: The German army was going to invade Poland—all missionaries were to be evacuated immediately.

By Friday, August 25, M. Douglas Wood, the president of the West German Mission, had sent telegrams to all the missionaries telling them to travel directly to the U.S. consulate in Rotterdam, Holland. However, later that day, word reached President Wood that despite the earlier permission of the Dutch consul, officials at the Dutch border were refusing entry to anyone who did not have tickets through to England. Eighty-four missionaries were on their way to the border with no money and no tickets.

The situation became even more tense by Saturday, August 26. No telephone or telegram service was available. Gas rationing meant that there was little or no transportation, and it was announced that by 10:00 P.M. the rail service was to be taken over by the military.

Lack of communication, transportation, food, and money were only a few of the challenges facing the missionaries. Many underwent Nazi interrogation, harassment, or detention. But each one also experienced undeniable miracles that ultimately secured their safe passage out of Germany. Among the amazing accounts recorded by these missionaries is the story of an Idaho missionary named Norman Seibold.

Upon receiving the telegram from his mission president, Elder Seibold left his area in Stuttgart and arrived at the mission home in Frankfurt on Saturday, August 26. As the crisis at the Dutch border unfolded, he volunteered to help find the missing missionaries.

President Wood gave Elder Seibold an envelope containing five hundred marks and tickets to London and Copenhagen. His charge was to travel the railway lines along the Dutch border and search for stranded missionaries.

It was dark by the time Elder Seibold boarded the train. He arrived in Cologne at 4:00 A.M., and despite the crowd's curious stares, he stood on a baggage cart and began whistling "Do What Is Right." He repeated this exercise at any station where he felt prompted to disembark the train.

On Monday, August 28, Elder Seibold saw thirteen of his fellow elders safely into Padborg, Denmark.

Then, because he couldn't be certain that he had found all the missing missionaries, Elder Seibold boarded a southbound train and headed back into Germany.

He found two more missionaries and sent them on to Denmark. Then he continued his search for another twenty-four hours.

After traveling on overcrowded trains with no sleep and very little to eat, he was at last prompted that he had fulfilled his responsibility.

He returned to Denmark on Tuesday, August 29, and was greeted with open arms by his mission president. With Elder Seibold's return, every missionary was safe and accounted for.

On Friday, September 1, 1939, the Nazis marched into Poland. By Sunday, September 3, Great Britain had declared war on Germany, and within hours France followed suit. World War II had begun.

SOURCES

Montague, Terry Bohle. *Mine Angels Round About: The Mormon Missionary Evacuation from West Germany, 1939.* Orem, UT: Granite, 2000.

Scharffs, Gilbert W. *Mormonism in Germany: A History of The Church of Jesus Christ of Latter-day Saints in Germany between 1840 and 1970.* Salt Lake City: Deseret Book, 1970.

Whiting, Charles. *The Home Front: Germany.* Alexandria, VA: Time-Life Books, 1982.

ABOUT THE AUTHOR

Siân Ann Bessey was born in Cambridge, England, to Noel and Patricia Owen. After her father completed his doctoral work there, the family returned to their Welsh homeland. Siân grew up among the austere mountains and verdant hills of North Wales. At the age of ten, she joined the Church along with her entire family. Siân left Wales to attend Brigham Young University and graduated with a bachelor's degree in communications.

In addition to her two novels, *Forgotten Notes* and *Cover of Darkness*, and her recent children's book, *A Family Is Forever*, Siân has written several articles that have appeared in the *New Era*, *Ensign*, and *Liahona* magazines.

Siân and her husband, Kent, are the parents of five children. They reside in Rexburg, Idaho.

Siân enjoys hearing from readers. You may write to her c/o Covenant Communications, P.O. Box 416, American Fork, UT 84003-0416, or e-mail her via Covenant at: info@covenant-lds.com.

Siân is the Welsh form of Jane and is pronounced "Shawn."